Carlos & Carmen

Fenced In

by Kirsten McDonald
illustrated by Fátima Anaya

Calico Kid

An Imprint of Magic Wagon
abdobooks.com

For the students at Emma Elementary and all of their families —KKM

To Angel, my baby brother who isn't a baby anymore but we still laughing of our childhood memories. —FA

abdobooks.com

Published by Magic Wagon, a division of ABDO, PO Box 398166, Minneapolis, Minnesota 55439. Copyright © 2020 by Abdo Consulting Group, Inc. International copyrights reserved in all countries. No part of this book may be reproduced in any form without written permission from the publisher. Calico Kid™ is a trademark and logo of Magic Wagon.

Printed in the United States of America, North Mankato, Minnesota.
052019
092019

Written by Kirsten McDonald
Illustrated by Fátima Anaya
Edited by Bridget O'Brien
Design Contributors: Christina Doffing & Candice Keimig

Library of Congress Control Number: 2018964637

Publisher's Cataloging-in-Publication Data

Names: McDonald, Kirsten, author. | Anaya, Fátima, illustrator.
Title: Fenced in / by Kirsten McDonald; illustrated by Fátima Anaya.
Description: Minneapolis, Minnesota : Magic Wagon, 2020. | Series: Carlos & Carmen
Summary: Carlos and Carmen are tired of having to wait for their parents to walk them to their neighbor Lola's house, until the three of them come up with the perfect solution.
Identifiers: ISBN 9781532134937 (lib. bdg.) | ISBN 9781532135538 (ebook) | ISBN 9781532135835 (Read-to-Me ebook)
Subjects: LCSH: Hispanic American families--Juvenile fiction. | Twins--Juvenile fiction. | Brothers and sisters--Juvenile fiction. | Patience--Juvenile fiction.
Classification: DDC [E]--dc23

Table of Contents

Chapter 1
Not Right Now

Carmen slipped on her space helmet.

"How does it look?" she asked her twin.

"¡Perfecto!" Carlos said. "What about my casco?"

"¡Muy perfecto!" said Carmen.

The twins raced into the kitchen. Mamá was working under the sink. Papá was holding a bunch of tools.

"Will you take us to Lola's casa, Mamá?" Carlos asked.

"Not right now," Mamá said. "I'm fixing the sink."

"How about you, Papá?" Carmen asked.

"Not right now," said Papá. "I'm helping fix the sink. Besides, you just got back from Lola's house."

"But we weren't finished playing," said Carlos.

"And we only came to our casa for lunch," said Carmen.

"And to make cascos," added Carlos.

Papá handed Mamá a wrench. He said, "Lo siento. You'll just have to wait."

"Maybe we could walk ourselves over," said Carmen.

"Maybe when you're older," said Papá.

"But there are aceras all the way," said Carlos. He put his helmet down.

"And those sidewalks will be there when you're older," said Mamá.

"Please!" said Carlos.

"Pretty please!" added Carmen.

"Lo siento," said Mamá, "but you'll just have to wait."

Chapter 2
Astronauts & Aliens

Carlos and Carmen leaned against the backyard fence. Through the cracks, they saw Lola and Moon walking toward them.

Lola was wearing purple pajamas and boots. She was also wearing a hat with a curly antenna.

"Bee bittle bot," Lola shouted.

"Over here!" Carmen shouted back. "At the cerca."

"She means at the fence!" added Carlos.

"Bop bop bee bee?" Lola asked as she walked to the fence.

"Not right now," said Carmen. "Our parents are busy."

"And, we're not allowed to walk by ourselves," added Carlos.

"Can you come to our house?" Carmen asked.

Lola took off her hat and shook her head.

"I already asked," Lola said. "Everybody's busy, so I have to wait until later."

"But it's no fun playing with a cerca between us," said Carmen.

"It's no fun waiting," said Carlos.

"And, it's no fun not having fun," added Lola.

It was a problem. A no-fun, hate-to-wait problem.

"What we need is a way to get over this cerca," said Carmen.

She jumped but could not reach the top of the fence.

"Or a way to get under it," said Lola, looking for a hole.

"Or a way to get through it," said Carlos, pushing on the boards.

Suddenly he stopped pushing.

Then Carlos looked at Carmen.

And, Carmen looked at Carlos.

"Are you thinking what I'm thinking?" they said. And because they were twins, they were.

Chapter 3
The Perfect Idea

Lola, however, was not a twin. She had to ask, "What are you thinking?"

"We need a puerta," said Carmen.

"She means a door," added Carlos. "In the cerca."

21

"So we can come to your house whenever we want," said Carmen.

"And you can come to our house whenever you want," added Carlos.

"That's perfect!" said Lola, tossing her hat in the air.

"¡Muy perfecto!" said Carlos, tossing his helmet in the air.

"¡Muy, muy perfecto!" added Carmen. Then she caught her twin's helmet. They ran to their house.

"¡Mamá! ¡Papá!" they yelled as they dashed into the kitchen. "We need your help!"

"¡Mis hijos!" said Mamá, putting away her tools. "What is wrong?"

"Nothing is wrong," said Carmen. She pounced on Papá's back.

"We have an idea that's perfecta," said Carlos, piling on top.

"An idea that's muy perfecta," added Carmen.

"We need your help," said Carlos.

They slipped off Papá's back. They told Mamá and Papá all about their idea for a door in the fence.

"Can we build it?" asked Carlos.

"Can we? Can we?" added Carmen.

"It might work," said Papá. He turned to Mamá and asked, "What do you think?"

Mamá lifted her toolbox and smiled. She said, "Looks like we've got something else to fix."

Chapter 4
The Perfect Door

For the rest of the afternoon, everyone worked. They measured and sawed. They hammered and painted.

Lola's mom came out with cookies for everyone. And, when the cookies were gone, she helped too.

Finally, the door was ready.

"Let's go to Lola's house," said Carlos. He opened the door, and everybody stepped into Lola's backyard.

"Now let's go to your house," said Lola. She opened the door, and everyone stepped back into the Garcias' backyard.

"It's perfecto!" said Carlos. "Now we can go to your house whenever we want."

"And I can go to your house whenever I want," said Lola.

Something scratched at the perfect door. It said, "Meow." A second later, something else said, "Murr-uhhh."

"I think I know who that is," said Carmen. She opened the door. Spooky and Moon walked through.

"I think I know one last thing this perfect puerta needs," said Mamá.

She took out her saw. She cut a cat-sized hole in the door.

Then everyone stood back and admired their work. The people smiled, and the cats smoothed their whiskers. And, they all agreed that they had built the perfect door.

Spanish to English

aceras – sidewalks

casa – house

casco – helmet

cerca – fence

Lo siento – I'm sorry

Mamá – Mommy

mis hijos – my children

muy – very

Papá – Daddy

perfecto/perfecta – perfect

puerta – door